THE WIND PEOPLE

Start Publishing PD is a registered trademark of Start Publishing PD LLC
Manufactured in the United States of America

Cover art: Shutterstock/Taisiya Kozorez

Cover design: Jennifer Do

10 9 8 7 6 5 4 3 2 1

ISBN 979-8-8809-2263-5

THE WIND PEOPLE

by Marion Zimmer Bradley

It had been a long layover for the *Starholm*'s crew, hunting heavy elements for fuel—eight months, on an idyllic green paradise of a planet; a soft, windy, whispering world, inhabited only by trees and winds. But in the end it presented its own unique problem. Specifically, it presented Captain Merrihew with the problem of Robin, male, father unknown, who had been born the day before, and a month prematurely, to Dr. Helen Murray.

Merrihew found her lying abed in the laboratory shelter, pale and calm, with the child beside her.

The little shelter, constructed roughly of green planks, looked out on the clearing which the *Starholm* had used as a base of operations during the layover; a beautiful place at the bottom of a wide valley, in the curve of a broad, deep-flowing river. The crew, tired of being shipbound, had built half a dozen such huts and shacks in these eight months.

Merrihew glared down at Helen. He snorted, "This is a fine situation. You, of all the people in the whole damned crew—the ship's doctor! It's—it's—" Inarticulate with rage, he fell back on a ridiculously inadequate phrase. "It's—criminal carelessness!"

"I know." Helen Murray, too young and far too lovely for a ship's officer on a ten-year cruise, still looked weak and white, and her voice was a gentle shadow of its crisp self.

"I'm afraid four years in space made me careless."

Merrihew, brooded, looking down at her. Something about ship—gravity conditions, while not affecting potency, made conception impossible; no child had ever been conceived in space and none ever would. On planet layovers, the effect wore off very slowly; only after three months aground had Dr. Murray started routine administration of anticeptin to the twenty-two women of the crew, herself included. At that time she had been still unaware that she herself was already carrying a child.

Outside, the leafy forest whispered and rustled, and Merrihew knew Helen had forgotten his existence again. The day-old child was tucked up in one of her rolled coveralls at her side. To Merrihew, he looked like a skinned monkey, but Helen's eyes smoldered as her hands moved gently over the tiny round head.

He stood and listened to the winds and said at random, "These shacks will fall to pieces in another month. It doesn't matter, we'll have taken off by then."

Dr. Chao Lin came into the shack, an angular woman of thirty-five. She said, "Company, Helen? Well, it's about time. Here, let me take Robin."

Helen said in weak protest, "You're spoiling me, Lin."

"It will do you good," Chao Lin returned. Merrihew, in a sudden surge of fury and frustration, exploded. "Damn it, Lin, you're making it all worse. He'll die when we go into overdrive, you know, as well as I do!"

Helen sat up, clutching Robin protectively. "Are you proposing to drown him like a kitten?"

THE WIND PEOPLE

"Helen, I'm not proposing anything. I'm stating a fact."

"But it's not a fact. He won't die in overdrive because he won't be aboard when we go into overdrive!"

Merrihew looked at Lin helplessly, but his face softened. "Shall we—put him to sleep and bury him here?"

The woman's face turned white. "No!" she cried in passionate protest, and Lin bent to disengage her frantic grip.

"Helen, you'll hurt him. Put him down. There." Merrihew looked down at her, troubled, and said, "We can't just abandon him to die slowly, Helen—"

"Who says I'm going to abandon him?" Merrihew asked slowly, "Are you planning to desert?" He added, after a minute, "There's a chance he'll survive. After all, his very birth was against all medical precedent. Maybe—"

"Captain"—Helen's voice sounded desperate—"even drugged, no child under ten has ever endured the shift into hyperspace drive. A newborn would die in seconds." She clasped Robin to her again and said, "It's the only way—you have Lin for a doctor, Reynolds can handle my collateral duties. This planet is uninhabited, the climate is mild, and we couldn't possibly starve." Her face, so gentle, was suddenly like rock. "Enter my death in the log, if you want to."

Merrihew looked from Helen to Lin, and said, "Helen, you're insane!"

She said, "Even if I'm sane now, I wouldn't be long if I had to abandon Robin." The wild note had died out of her voice, and she spoke rationally, but inflexibly. "Captain Merrihew, to get me aboard the *Starholm*, you will have to have me drugged or taken by force; I promise you I won't go any other way. And if you do that—and if Robin is left behind, or dies in overdrive, just so you will have my services as a doctor—then I solemnly swear that I will kill myself at the first opportunity."

"My God," said Merrihew, "you are insane!"

Helen gave a very tiny shrug. "Do you want a madwoman aboard?" Chao Lin said quietly, "Captain, I don't see any other way. We would have had to arrange it that way if Helen had actually died in childbirth. Of two unsatisfactory solutions, we must choose the less harmful." And Merrihew knew that he had no real choice. "I still think you're both crazy," he blustered, but it was surrender, and Helen knew it. Ten days after the *Starholm* took off, young Colin Reynolds, technician, committed suicide by the messy procedure of slicing his jugular vein, which—in zero gravity—distributed several quarts of blood in big round globules all over his cabin. He left an incoherent note.

THE WIND PEOPLE

Merrihew put the note in the disposal and Chao Lin put the blood in the ship's blood bank for surgery, and they hushed it up as an accident; but Merrihew had the unpleasant feeling that the layover on the green and windy planet was going to become a legend, spread in whispers by the crew. And it did, but that is another story.

Robin was two years old when he first heard the voices in the wind. He pulled at his mother's arms and crooned softly, in imitation.

"What is it, lovey?"

"Pretty." He crooned again to the distant murmuring sound. Helen smiled vaguely and patted the round cheek. Robin, his infant imagination suddenly distracted, said, "Hungry. Robin hungry. Berries."

"Berries after you eat," Helen promised absently, and picked him up. Robin tugged at her arm.

"Mommy pretty, too!"

She laughed, a rosy and smiling young Diana. She was happy on the solitary planet; they lived quite comfortably in one of the larger shacks, and only a little frown line between her eyes bore witness to the terror which had closed down on her in the first months, when every new day had been some new struggle—against weakness, against unfamiliar sounds, against loneliness and dread. Nights when she lay wakeful, sweating with terror while the winds rose and fell again and her imagination gave them voices, bleak days when she wandered dazedly around the shack or stared moodily at Robin. There had been moments—only fleeting, and penanced with hours of shame and regret—when she thought that even the horror of losing Robin in those first days would have been less than the horror of spending the rest of her life alone here, when she had wondered why Merrihew had not realized that she was unbalanced, and forced her to go with them; by now, Robin would have been only a moment's painful memory.

Still not strong, knowing she had to be strong for Robin or he would die as surely as if she had abandoned him, she had spent the first months in a somnambulistic dream.

Sometimes she had walked for days at a time in that dream; she would wake to find food that she could not remember gathering. Somehow, pervasive, the dream voices had taken over; the whispering winds had been full of voices and even hands.

She had fallen ill and lain for days sick and delirious, and had heard a voice which hardly seemed to be her own, saying that if she died the wind voices would care for Robin . . . and then the shock and irrationality of that had startled her out of delirium, agonized and trembling, and she pulled herself upright and cried out, "No!"

THE WIND PEOPLE

And the shimmer of eyes and voices had faded again into vague echoes, until there was only the stir of sunlight on the leaves, and Robin, chubby and naked, kicking in the sunlight, cooing with his hands outstretched to the rustle of leaves and shadows.

She had known, then, that she had to get well. She had never heard the wind voices again, and her crisp, scientific mind rejected the fanciful theory that if she only believed in the wind voices she would see their forms and hear their words clearly. And she rejected them so thoroughly that when she heard them speak, she shut them away from her mind, and after a time heard them no longer, except in restless dreams.

By now she had accepted the isolation and the beauty of their world, and begun to make a happy life for Robin.

For lack of other occupation last summer—though the winter was mild and there was no lack of fruits and roots even then—Helen had patiently snared male and female of small animals like rabbits, and now she had a pen of them. They provided a change of diet, and after a few smelly unsuccessful experiments she had devised a way to supply their fur pelts. She made no effort at gardening, though when Robin was older she might try that. For the moment, it was enough that they were healthy and safe and protected.

Robin was listening again. Helen bent her ear, sharpened by the silence, but heard only the rustle of wind and leaves; saw only falling brightness along a silvered tree-trunk. Wind? When there were no branches stirring?

"Ridiculous," she said sharply, then snatched up the baby boy and squeezed him before hoisting him astride her hip. "Mommy doesn't mean you, Robin. Let's look for berries."

But soon she realized that his head was tipped back and that he was listening, again, to some sound she could not hear.

On what she said was Robin's fifth birthday, Helen had made a special bed for him in another room of the building. He missed the warmth of Helen's body, and the comforting sound of her breathing; for Robin, since birth, had been a wakeful child.

Yet, on the first night alone, Robin felt curiously freed. He did something he had never dared do before, for fear of waking Helen; he slipped from his bed and stood in the doorway, looking into the forest.

The forest was closer to the doorway now; Robin could fuzzily remember when the clearing had been wider. Now, slowly, beyond the garden patch which Helen kept cleared, the underbrush and saplings were growing back, and even what Robin called "the burned place" was covered with new sparse grass.

Robin was accustomed to being alone during the day—even in his first year, Helen had had to leave him alone, securely fastened in the house, or inside a little tight-fenced yard. But he was not used to being alone at night.

Far off in the forest, he could hear the whispers of the other people. Helen said there were no other people, but Robin knew better, because he could hear their voices on the wind, like fragments of the songs Helen sang at bedtime. And sometimes he could almost see them in the shadowy spots.

Once when Helen had been sick, a long time ago, and Robin had run helplessly from the fenced yard to the inside room and back again, hungry and dirty and furious because Helen only slept on the bed with her eyes closed, rousing up now and then to whimper like he did when he fell down and skinned his knee, the winds and voices had come into the very house; Robin had hazy memories of soothing voices, of hands that touched him more softly than Helen's hands. But he could not quite remember.

Now that he could hear them so clearly, he would go and find the other people. And then if Helen was sick again, there would be someone else to play with him and look after him. He thought gleefully, *Won't Helen be surprised?* and darted off across the clearing.

Helen woke, roused not by a sound but by a silence. She no longer heard Robin's soft breaths from the alcove, and after a moment she realized something else: The winds were silent.

Perhaps, she thought, a storm was coming. Some change in air pressure could cause this stillness—but Robin? She tiptoed to the alcove; as she had suspected, his bed was empty.

Where could he be? In the clearing? With a storm coming? She slid her feet into handmade sandals and ran outside, her quivering call ringing out through the silent forest: "Robin—oh, Robin!"

Silence. And far away a little ominous whisper. And for the first time since that first frightening year of loneliness, she felt lost, deserted in an alien world. She ran across the clearing, looking around wildly, trying to decide which way he could have wandered. Into the forest? What if he had strayed toward the riverbank? There was a place where the bank crumbled away, down toward the rapids—her throat closed convulsively, and her call was almost a shriek: "Oh, Robin! Robin, darling! Robin!"

She ran through the paths worn by then—feet, hearing snatches of rustle, winds and leaves suddenly vocal in the cold moonlight around her. It was the first time since the spaceship left them that Helen had ventured out into the night of their world. She called again, her voice cracking in panic.

"Robin!"

A sudden stray gleam revealed a glint of white, and a child stood in the middle of the path. Helen gasped with relief and ran to snatch up her son—then fell back in dismay. It was not Robin who stood there. The child was naked, about a head shorter than Robin, and female.

There was something curious about the bare and gleaming flesh, as if she could see the child only hi the full flush of the moonlight. A round, almost expressionless face was surrounded by a mass of colorless streaming hair, the exact color of the moonlight. Helen's audible gasp startled her to a stop: she shut her eyes convulsively, and when she opened them the path was black and empty and Robin was running down the track toward her.

Helen caught him up, with a strangled cry, and ran, clasping him to her breast, back down the path to their shack. Inside, she barred the door and laid Robin down in her own bed, and threw herself down shivering, too shaken to speak, too shaken to scold him, curiously afraid to question. I had a hallucination, she told herself, a hallucination, another dream, a dream. . .

A dream, like the other Dream. She signified it to herself as The Dream because it was not like any other dream she had ever had. She had dreamed it first before Robin's birth, and been ashamed to speak of it to Chao Lin, fearing the common-sense skepticism of the older woman.

On their tenth night on the green planet (the *Starholm* was a dim recollection now), when

Mernhew's scientists had been convinced that the little world was safe, without wild beasts or diseases or savage natives, the crew had requested permission to camp in the valley clearing beside the river. Permission granted, they had gone apart in couples almost as usual, and even those who had no enduring liaison at the moment had found a partner for the night.

It must have been that night...

Colin Reynolds was two years younger than Helen, and their attachment, enduring over a few months of ship time, was based less on mutual passion than on a sort of boyish need in him, a sort of impersonal feminine solicitude in Helen. All her affairs had been like that, companionable, comfortable, but never passionate. Curiously enough, Helen was a woman capable of passion, of great depths of devotion; but no man had ever roused it and now no man ever would. Only Robin's birth had touched her deeply pent emotions.

But that night, when Colin Reynolds was sleeping, Helen stayed restlessly awake, hearing the unquiet stirring of wind on the leaves. After a time she wandered down to the water's edge, staying a cautious distance from the shore—for the cliff crumbled dangerously—and stretched herself out to listen to the wind—voices. And after a time she fell asleep, and had The Dream, which was to return to her again and again.

Helen thought of herself as a scientist, without room for fantasies, and that was why she called it, fiercely, a dream; a dream born of some undiagnosed conflict in her. Even to herself Helen would not recall it in full.

There had been a man, and to her it seemed that he was part of the green and windy world, and he had found her sleeping by the river. Even in her drowsy state, Helen had suspected that perhaps one of the other crew members, like herself sleepless and drawn to the shining water, had happened upon her there, such things were not impossible, manners and mores being what they were among starship crew's.

But to her, half dreaming, there had been some strangeness about him, which prevented her from seeing him too clearly even in the brilliant green moonlight. No dream and no man had ever seemed so living to her; and it was her fierce rationalization of the dream which kept her silent, months later, when she discovered (to her horror and secret despair) that she was with child. She had felt that she would lose the haze and secret delight of the dream if she openly acknowledged that Colin had fathered her child. But at first—in the cool green morning that followed—she had not been at all sure it was a dream. Seeing only sunlight and leaves, she had held back from speaking, not wanting ridicule; could she have asked each man of the *Starholm*, "Was it you who came to me last night? Because if it was not, there are other men on this world, men who cannot be clearly seen even by moonlight."

Severely she reminded herself, Merrihew's men had pronounced the world uninhabited, and uninhabited it must be. Five years later, hugging her sleeping son close, Helen remembered the dream, examined the content of her fantasy, and once again, shivering, repeated, "I had a hallucination. It was only a dream. A dream, because I was alone ..." When Robin was fourteen years old, Helen told him the story of his birth, and of the ship. He was a tall, silent boy, strong and hardy but not talkative; he heard the story almost in silence, and looked at Helen for a long time in silence afterward. He finally said in a whisper, "You could have died—you gave up a lot for me, Helen, didn't you?" He knelt and took her face in his hands.

She smiled and drew a little away from him. "Why are you looking at me like that, Robin?"

The boy could not put instant words to his thoughts; emotions were not in his vocabulary. Helen had taught him everything she knew, but she had always concealed her feelings from her son. He asked at last, "Why didn't my father stay with you?"

THE WIND PEOPLE

"I don't suppose it entered his head," Helen said. "He was needed on the ship. Losing me was bad enough."

Robin said passionately, "I'd have stayed!"

The woman found herself laughing. "Well—you did stay, Robin."

He asked, "Am I like my father?"

Helen looked gravely at her son, trying to see the half-forgotten features of young Reynolds in the boy's face. No, Robin did not look like Colin Reynolds, nor like Helen herself. She picked up his hand in hers; despite his robust health, Robin never tanned; his skin was pearly pale, so that in the green sunlight it blended into the forest almost invisibly. His hand lay in Helen's palm like a shadow. She said at last, "No, nothing like him. But under this sun, that's to be expected."

Robin said confidently, "I'm like the *other* people."

"The ones on the ship? They—"

"No," Robin interrupted, "you always said when I was older you'd tell me about the other people. I mean the other people here. The ones in the woods. The ones you can't see."

Helen stared at the boy in blank disbelief. "What do you mean? There are no other people, just us." Then she recalled that every imaginative child invents playmates. Alone, she thought, *Robin's always alone, no other children, no wonder he's a little—strange.* She said quietly, "You dreamed it, Robin."

The boy only stared at her in bleak, blank alienation. "You mean," he said, "you can't *hear* them, either?" He got up and walked out of the hut. Helen called, but he didn't turn back. She ran after him, catching at his arm, stopping him almost by force. She whispered, "Robin, Robin, tell me what you mean! There isn't anyone here. Once or twice I thought I had seen—something, by moonlight, only it was a dream. Please, Robin—please—"

"If it's only a dream, why are you frightened?" Robin asked, through a curious constriction in his throat. "If they've never hurt you ..."

No, they had never hurt her. Even if, in her long-ago dream, one of them had come to her. *And the sons of God saw the daughters of men that they were fair*—a scrap of memory from a vanished life on another world sang in Helen's thoughts. She looked up at the pale, impatient face of her son, and swallowed hard.

Her voice was husky when she spoke. "Did I ever tell you about rationalization—when you want something to be true so much that you can make it sound right to yourself?"4

"Couldn't that also happen to something you wanted not to be true?" Robin retorted with a mutinous curl of his mouth.

THE WIND PEOPLE

Helen would not let go his arm. She begged, "Robin, no, you'll only waste your life and break your heart looking for something that doesn't exist."

The boy looked down into her shaken face, and suddenly a new emotion welled up in him and he dropped to his knees beside her and buried his face against her breast. He whispered, "Helen, I'll never leave you, I'll never do anything you don't want me to do, I don't want anyone but you."

And for the first time in many years, Helen broke into wild and uncontrollable crying, without knowing why she wept.

Robin did not speak again of his quest in the forest. For many months he was quiet and subdued, staying near the clearing, hovering near Helen for days at a time, then disappearing into the forest at dusk. He heard the winds numbly, deaf to their promise and their call.

Helen too was quiet and withdrawn, feeling Robin's alienation through his submissive mood. She found herself speaking to him sharply for being always underfoot; yet, on the rare days when he vanished into the forest and did not return until after sunset, she felt a restless unease that set her wandering the paths herself, not following him, but simply uneasy unless she knew he was within call.

Once, in the shadows just before sunset, she thought she saw a man moving through the trees, and for an instant, as he turned toward her, she saw that he was naked. She had seen him only for a second or two, and after he had slipped between the shadows again common sense told her it was Robin. She was vaguely shocked and annoyed; she firmly intended to speak to him, perhaps to scold him for running about naked and slipping away like that; then, in a sort of remote embarrassment, she forbore to mention it. But after that, she kept out of the forest.

Robin had been vaguely aware of her surveillance and knew when it ceased. But he did not give up his own pointless rambles, although even to himself he no longer spoke of searching, or of any dreamlike inhabitants of the woods. At tunes it still seemed that some shadow concealed a half-seen form, and the distant murmur grew into a voice that mocked him; a white arm, the shadow of a face, until he lifted his head and stared straight at it.

One evening toward twilight he saw a sudden shimmer in the trees, and he stood, fixedly, as the stray glint resolved itself first into a white face with shadowy eyes, then into a translucent flicker of bare arms, and then into the form of a woman, arrested for an instant with her hand on the bole of a tree. In the shadowy spot, filled only with the last ray of a cloudy sunset, she was very clear; not cloudy or unreal, but so distinct that he could see even a small smudge, or bramble scratch on her shoulder, and a fallen leaf tangled in her colorless hair. Robin, paralyzed, watched her pause, and turn, and smile, and then she melted into the shadows.

He stood with his heart pouncing for a second after she had gone; then whirled, bursting with the excitement of his discovery, and ran down the path toward home. Suddenly he stopped short, the world tilting and reeling, and fell on his face in a bed of dry leaves.

He was still ignorant of the nature of the emotion in him. He felt only intolerable misery and the conviction that he must never, never speak to Helen of what he had seen or felt. He lay there, his burning face pressed into the leaves, unaware of the rising wind, the little flurry of blown leaves, the growing darkness and distant thunder. At last an icy spatter of rain aroused him, and cold, numbed, he made his way slowly homeward. Over his head the boughs creaked woodenly, and Robin, under the driving whips of the rain, felt their tumult only echoed his own voiceless agony.

He was drenched by the time he pushed the door of the shack open and stumbled blindly toward the fire, only hoping that Helen would be sleeping. But she started up from beside the hearth they had built together last summer.

"Robin?" Deathly weary, the boy snapped, "Who *else* would it be?"

Helen didn't answer. She came to him, a small swift-moving figure in the firelight, and drew him into the warmth. She said, almost humbly, "I was afraid—the storm—Robin, you're all wet, come to the fire and dry out."

Robin yielded, his twitching nerves partly soothed by her voice. *How tiny Helen is,* he thought, *and I can remember that she used to carry me around on one arm; now she hardly comes to my shoulder.* She brought him food and he ate wolfishly, listening to the steady pouring rain, uncomfortable under Helen's watching eyes. Before his own eyes there was the clear memory of the woman in the wood, and so vivid was Robin's imagination, heightened by loneliness and undiluted by any random impressions, that it seemed to him Helen must see her too. And when she came to stand beside him, the picture grew so keen in his thoughts that he actually pulled himself free of her.

The next day dawned gray and still, beaten with long needles of rain. They stayed indoors by the smoldering fire; Robin, half sick and feverish from his drenching, sprawled by the hearth too indolent to move, watching Helen's comings and goings about the room; not realizing why the sight of her slight, quick form against the gray fight filled him with such pain and melancholy.

The storm lasted four days. Helen exhausted her household tasks and sat restlessly thumbing through the few books she knew by heart—they had allowed her to remove all her personal possessions, all the things she had chosen on a forgotten and faraway Earth for a ten-year star cruise. For the first time in years, Helen was thinking again of the life, the civilization she had thrown away, for Robin who had been a pink scrap in the circle of her arm and now lay sullen on the hearth, not speaking, aimlessly whittling a stick with a knife (found discarded in a heap of rubbish from the *Starholm*) which was his dearest possession. Helen felt slow horror closing in on her. *What world, what heritage did I give him, in my madness? This world has driven us both insane. Robin and I are both a little mad, by Earth's standard's. And when I die, and I will die first, what then?* At that moment Helen would have given her life to believe in his old dream of strange people in the wood.

She flung her book restlessly away, and Robin, as if waiting for that signal, sat upright and said almost eagerly, "Helen—"

Grateful that he had broken the silence of days, she gave him an encouraging smile.

"I've been reading your books," he began diffidently, "and I read about the sun you came from. It's different from this one. Suppose—suppose there were actually a kind of people here, and something in this light, or in your eyes, made them invisible to you."

Helen said, "Have you been seeing them again?"

He flinched at her ironical tone, and she asked, somewhat more gently, "It's a theory, Robin, but it wouldn't explain, then, *why* you see them."

"Maybe I'm—more used to this light," he said gropingly. "And anyway, you said you thought you'd seen them and thought it was only a dream."

Halfway between exasperation and a deep pity, Helen found herself arguing, "If these other people of yours really exist, why haven't they made themselves known in sixteen years?

The eagerness with which he answered was almost frightening. "I think they only come out at night, they're what your book calls a primitive civilization." He spoke the words he had read, but never heard, with an odd hesitation. "They're not really a civilization at all, I think, they're like—part of the woods."

"A forest people," Helen mused, impressed in spite of herself, "and nocturnal. It's always moonlight or dusky when you see them—"

"Then you *do* believe me—oh, Helen," Robin cried, and suddenly found himself pouring out the story of what he had seen, in incoherent words, concluding, "and by daylight I can hear them, but I can't see them. Helen, Helen, you have to believe it now, you'll have to let me try to find them and learn to talk to them ..."

THE WIND PEOPLE

Helen listened with a sinking heart. She knew they should not discuss it now, when five days of enforced housebound proximity had set their nerves and tempers on edge, but some unknown tension hurled her words at Robin. "You saw a woman, and I—a man. These things are only dreams. Do I have to explain more to you?"

Robin flung his knife sullenly aside. "You're so blind, so stubborn."

"I think you are feverish again." Helen rose to go.

He said wrathfully, "You treat me like a child!"

"Because you act like one, with your fairy tales of women in the wind."

Suddenly Robin's agony overflowed and he caught at her, holding her around the knees, clinging to her as he had not done since he was a small child, his words stumbling and rushing over one another.

"Helen, Helen darling, don't be angry with me," he begged, and caught her in a blind embrace that pulled her off her feet. She had never guessed how strong he was; but he seemed very like a little boy, and she hugged him quickly as he began to cover her face with childish kisses.

"Don't cry, Robin, my baby, it's all right," she murmured, kneeling close to him.

Gradually the wildness of his passionate crying abated; she touched his forehead with her cheek to see if it was heated with fever, and he reached up and held her there. Helen let him lie against her shoulder, feeling that perhaps after the violence of his outburst he would fall asleep, and she was half-asleep herself when a sudden shock of realization darted through her; quickly she tried to free herself from Robin's entangling arms.

"Robin, let me go."

He clung to her, not understanding. "Don't let go of me, Helen. Darling, stay here beside me," he begged, and pressed a kiss into her throat.

Helen, her blood icing over, realized that unless she freed herself very quickly now, she would be fighting against a strong, aroused young man not clearly aware of what he was doing. She took refuge in the sharp maternal note of ten years ago, almost vanished in the closer, more equal companionship of the time between: "No, Robin. Stop it at once, do you hear?"

Automatically he let her go, and she rolled quickly away, out of his reach, and got to her feet. Robin, too intelligent to be unaware of her anger and too naive to know its cause, suddenly dropped his head and wept, wholly unstrung. "Why are you angry?" he blurted out. "I was only loving you."

And at the phrase of the five-year-old child, Helen felt her throat would burst with its ache. She managed to choke out, "I'm not angry, Robin—we'll talk about this later, I promise," and then, her own control vanishing, turned and fled precipitately into the pouring rain.

She plunged through the familiar woods for a long time, in a daze of unthinking misery. She did not even fully realize that she was sobbing and muttering aloud, "No, no, no, no!"

She must have wandered for several hours. The rain had stopped and the darkness was lifting before she began to grow calmer and to think more clearly.

She had been blind not to foresee this day when Robin was a child; only if her child had been a daughter could it have been avoided. Or—she was shocked at the hysterical sound of her own laughter—if Colin had stayed and they had raised a family like Adam and Eve!

But what now? Robin was sixteen; she was not yet forty. Helen caught at vanishing memories of society; taboos so deeply rooted that for Helen they were instinctual and impregnable. Yet for Robin nothing existed except this little patch of forest and Helen herself—the only person in his world, more specifically at the moment the only woman in his world. *So much,* she thought bitterly, *for instinct. But have I the right to begin this all over again? Worse; have I the right to deny its existence and, when I die, leave Robin alone?*

She had stumbled and paused for breath, realizing that she had wandered in circles and that she was at a familiar point on the riverbank which she had avoided for sixteen years. On the heels of this realization she became aware that for only the second time in memory, the winds were wholly stilled.

Her eyes, swollen with crying, ached as she tried to pierce the gloom of the mist, lilac-tinted with the approaching sunrise, which hung around the water. Through the dispersing mist she made out, dimly, the form of a man.

He was tall, and his pale skin shone with misty white colors. Helen sat frozen, her mouth open, and for the space of several seconds he looked down at her without moving. His eyes, dark splashes in the pale face, had an air of infinite sadness and compassion, and she thought his lips moved in speech, but she heard only a win familiar rustle of wind.

Behind him, mere flickers, she seemed to make out the ghosts of other faces, tips of fingers of invisible hands, eyes, the outline of a woman's breast, the curve of a child's foot. For a minute, in Helen's weary numbed state, all her defenses went down and she thought: *Then I'm not mad and it wasn't a dream and Robin isn't Reynolds' son at all. His father was Ms—one of these—and they've been watching me and Robin, Robin has seen them, he doesn't know he's one of them, but they know. They know and I've kept Robin from them all these sixteen years.*

The man took two steps toward her, the translucent body shifting to a dozen colors before her blurred eyes.

THE WIND PEOPLE

His face had a curious *familiarity*—familiarity—and in a sudden spasm of terror Helen thought, "I'm going mad, it's Robin, *its Robin!*"

His hand was actually outstretched to touch her when her scream cut icy lashes through the forest, stirring wild echoes in the wind-voices, and she whirled and ran blindly toward the treacherous, crumbling bank. Behind her came steps, a voice, a cry—Robin, the strange dryad-man, she could not guess. The horror of incest, the son the father the lover suddenly melting into one, overwhelmed her reeling brain and she fled insanely to the brink. She felt a masculine hand actually gripping her shoulder, she might have been pulled back even then, but she twisted free blindly, shrieking, "No, Robin, no, no—" and flung herself down the steep bank, to slip and hurl downward and whirl around in—the raging current to spinning oblivion and death . . .

Many years later, Merrihew, grown old in the Space Service, falsified a log entry to send his ship for a little while into the orbit of the tiny green planet he had named Robin's World. The old buildings had fallen into rotted timbers, and Merrihew quartered the little world for two months from pole to pole but found nothing. Nothing but shadows and whispers and the unending voices of the wind. Finally, he lifted his ship and went away.